UP IN THE MOUNTAIN

First Time MM Age Gap Story

Michael Levi

ISBN: 9798773643937
Imprint: Independently published

2nd edition

Cover design by: Michael Levi

TEASER

Mark felt how gentle James was. He remembered the charismatic, happy man that James had been. It was then that he realized he could change James and make him remember the man he was three years ago.

James sped up and pumped Mark harder when he felt that the young man had gotten used to his cock.

Mark felt James' balls constantly hitting against his ass.

Minutes went by until James reached his climax. His cock started to pulse and he got out of Mark's tight hole.

"Look at me," he commanded at the twink in front of him.

He got on his knees and readied himself for the cum shower. The first rope came out in high speed and hit his right cheek. Then, one after the other, James painted the young man's face.

Mark swallowed what he could and lied down on the floor. He had a smile on his face and looked happy.

He had finally come to terms with his life. He craved James, and the latter wanted him as well...

CONTENTS

Title Page

Copyright

Teaser

Chapter 1 — 1

Chapter 2 — 3

Chapter 3 — 5

Chapter 4 — 7

Chapter 5 — 11

Chapter 6 — 14

Chapter 7A — 16

Chapter 7B — 19

Chapter 7C — 23

Straight to Gay Series and More — 29

About the Author — 31

CHAPTER 1

It was 1992 and the internet was still not popular. James, a 40-year-old husband, had secretly bought a couple of gay magazines at the local store.

He knew that his wife couldn't know about them. She couldn't know that her loving hubby had eyes for men as well.

He did love her and he always made that clear when it was brought up. Their friends rolled their eyes at his enthusiasm.

His wife, Jelly, was at work. The one he looked after, Chris, was at school studying. That meant he had some free time to look at his magazines.

He opened a box he had left in the wardrobe and picked them. It wasn't the first time he was checking on the magazines, so they were a bit sticky.

He started flipping the pages and admiring the young men with their naked chests. His cock started to grow.

James had a fetish for younger men, especially the ones between the ages of 18 and 22. The magazines he'd bought featured only that kind of man.

Moments later, he put the magazines aside and flopped onto the bed. He used his imagination to finish things up.

Wild images and moments featuring those hot young men under him were enough to keep him going.

He started to masturbate faster and seconds later, he was blowing his load all over his belly.

He took long breaths and let his cock rest on his stomach. Then, he picked some tissue paper and cleaned himself up quickly.

He knew that Chris and his friend would soon be coming home.

They'd planned on traveling to the mountains and getting some nice, fresh air away from the city. He couldn't wait to finally have some free time away from his problems.

CHAPTER 2

Mark was an 18-year-old student at Primbroke College. He was seated in the bathroom stall. To anyone outside, he was just taking a dump. However, he was actually hiding from the students and professors.

Mark was a shy young man. James often to beat him up when he was pissed. Living near that man made him lose his self-esteem.

He had recently found out that he was gay. He started to develop feelings for his friends and professor. His history teacher, a tall and confident 30-year-old guy, was his crush.

His boner was showing up through his pants. He left the classroom as soon as his cock started to grow bigger. He wouldn't have been able to deal with the shame, had anyone looked at his crotch.

As soon as he calmed himself down, he walked out of the bathroom. The only good thing about that day, he thought, was that James was going to take the two of them to the mountain.

It was going to be the best time of his life, he thought. He wanted to get away from his school and parents' house for a couple of days.

Once the class was over, he said to Chris, "I can't wait to go to the mountain with James."

"Me too," Chris said, "I want to relax a little and breathe some fresh air from the forests. It's going to be cold, though."

"Yeah, I know about that,' Mark replied, "Which is why I brought some jackets and thick pants."

"Did you get some hiking equipment as well? I think we will need them."

"Sure I did. James said the trails are some of the best in the region."

"Yeah, he always says that. However, we should be careful; I have heard stories of accidents that happened on that mountain."

"Really? What happened there?"

"Well, that place is prone to landslides."

Shock crossed Mark's face.

"However," Chris said, "He is a pro. As long as we stick with him, nothing bad will happen."

"S- sure, I hope so," Mark replied, looking a bit scared.

"Yeah, don't worry," Chris said as he put his hands on the back of his head. "We won't be using the trails that often anyway."

They got inside the bus that was going to take them to Chris' house. Once they had everything packed in the car, James was going to take them to the mountain.

CHAPTER 3

T he two of them finally arrived, James thought as he looked at them getting out of the bus. He was at the door and had a jovial smile on his face.

"You're here, finally!" He exclaimed as he picked up Chris.

Chris looked uncomfortable for still being treated like that by James. Mark giggled a little.

James put his brat back on the ground and caressed Mark's head.

"Can we go now?" Chris asked. He looked annoyed.

"Sure. Grab your things and put them in the car."

Chris walked upstairs to pack his bags.

"And little Mark," James said, "Take your bag to the trunk of the car. I will open it for you."

"Okay!" Mark said.

Once they were done putting the bags in the car, James turned the engine on and headed towards the mountain.

"So, what is the mountain like?" Mark asked.

"You have never been there, right?" James said, "They are pretty cold this time of the year. There are some difficult trails, but nothing too dangerous."

"Tell him about the monsters," Chris said.

"Oh yeah, sometimes you can see a monster or two. They are usually pretty shy, though."

"We will be sleeping in a cabin," he continued, "I hope you two don't mind snoring. I snore quite a bit. Jelly hates me for that."

Once they got to the base of the mountain, James grabbed

their bags and began to carry them.

It was going to take a couple of hours to get to the cabin and the luggage was heavy, but James didn't mind any of that.

"Oh wow, this place looks awesome!" Mark said as his eyes flashed with excitement.

They had a great view of a large lake in the distance and the city. It all looked so distant and insignificant, James thought as he contemplated being away from his stressful life.

"This place is one of the most visited spots during the summer," James said, "It's the winter right now, so I'm going to be your only friend around here."

"That is why we came here," Chris said, "We want to spend some time away from society."

They continued their way up on the trail when the group spotted a small landslide in the distance. James said, "Gentlemen, that is why we shouldn't make too much noise."

"Yeah, we know," Chris said, looking uninterested.

Mark looked scared and advised, "The sooner we get to the cabin, the better. I don't feel safe on this trail anymore."

"Mark, really," Chris rolled his eyes, "we'll be fine. This old man here is a pro with hiking and chilling in this mountain."

Then, they finally reached the cabin. It looked old but sturdy. James grabbed the keys and opened the door. Then, he put the luggage on the floor and stretched his arms.

"Alright, you two," James said. "You need to shower before going to bed."

"Sure," Chris replied.

"Can I go first?" Mark asked, "I need to pee."

"Uh okay, sure," Chris replied, "Just be quick."

Mark grabbed some of his clothes and went to the bathroom. While he did want to pee, he didn't want to tell James and Chris the whole reason he went there.

He was, once again, developing feelings for people he shouldn't. That alone destroyed mental health, and he always needed a long, hot shower to recover.

CHAPTER 4

James woke up with a smile on his face. He had a good night's sleep and felt ready to hike.

He went to the kitchen and started preparing breakfast.

"Good morning!" James said as Chris walked in, "Do you want tea or hot chocolate today, my little prince?"

Chris looked groggy and said, "Stop saying those things to me. I'm an adult now."

"Not yet, my little prince," James said as he smiled at Chris and put a plate full of bacon and eggs on the table.

Then Mark came in, who was also looking groggy.

"What about you, little Mark?" James asked, "Do you also want bacon and eggs for your breakfast?"

Mark could barely think straight, but he said, "Y- yeah, they smell delicious."

James made some more bacon and eggs. He put a full plate in front of the young one as his eyes cherished the food in front of him.

Once they were done eating, they grabbed their hiking equipment and headed out. The dim light of the sun gave the atmosphere an eerie look, but it was not enough to diminish their excitement.

They took the trail that led farther up in the mountain. James' idea was to take them to have the best view of the region. Up there, they would have a 360o panorama of the valley.

"How long is the trip to the top?" Mark asked James.

"About an hour," he replied, "it's a little long, but we need to watch our step. This trail can be a little unforgiving."

As Mark walked on the trail, he began to notice James was right. More often than not, the path lacked safety barriers. Any misstep could mean his death, if he wasn't careful.

Chris, however, just wanted to get to the top. About halfway through there, he was already tired.

"How long until we get there?" Chris asked, looking irritated.

"Just a little bit more," James replied. "We'll rest up when we get there."

Once they arrived there, Chris was finally able to take in the beautiful view of the valley. He spotted the lake and the city in the distance.

"This place is beautiful," Chris said, "It feels so peaceful being here. I don't want to leave anytime soon."

"Sure. We should rest and appreciate the fresh air."

And up there they remained until it was getting dark. They played snowball fights and talked about funny moments that happened during the year. Before they realized it, the sun was already setting.

"Okay guys," James said while he stretched his arms, "Time to head back to the cabin. Tomorrow we will hike another trail."

"It won't be as exciting as this one," Chris said, looking uninterested.

"Who are you to say that?" James said, "You will be surprised with the secrets this mountain has."

"Yeah, Chris," Mark said, "Your father is right. Every trail is unique and I can't wait to try the next one tomorrow."

They started a heated discussion on their expectations for the next day. The tone of their voices got louder as they walked down the path.

Nobody noticed the falling snow on the underside of the path. When they were farther down the trail and surrounded by snow on all sides, they were too busy to notice the danger they were in.

James looked up as shock crossed his eyes. "Guys, stop!" He shouted and everyone stopped talking. The snow on their right side looked as if it was about to go down at any moment.

Mark looked scared and, at that moment, he was incapable of rational thinking. Instead of walking, he decided to run to the only one who could make him feel safe: James.

Mark's running footsteps were loud enough to release the avalanche.

James had no time to react when the snow rolled down. In a matter of seconds, it swallowed Chris whole.

The only thing he and Mark could do was to run. James grabbed Mark and carried him down away from the avalanche.

At that moment, neither James nor Mark had time to think about Chris. All they knew was that they needed to get to the cabin.

Once they reached the place, James put Mark on the couch and sat on the chair. He closed his eyes and didn't move a muscle for the next 10 minutes.

Mark was sitting on the couch, hugging his knees. He was looking at James, but James didn't want to say or do anything.

Then, he decided to break the silence. "I need to go out, Mark," he said with a tone of defeat in his voice. "You need to stay here. It's safe."

Mark didn't say anything and just looked at James. The latter opened his eyes and stood up, with a look of determination on his face. He knew he had failed Chris.

However, never once did he consider that Chris was already dead. No, that couldn't be possible, he thought.

The more he looked, all over the mountain, the more he concluded he truly failed Chris.

Not only that, but he realized that Mark and he couldn't leave the mountain. The avalanche had blocked the only trail to the road. He was going to have to wait for his wife to call the police and ask for his rescue.

He knew, also, that the cabin had no communication with the outside world. Likewise, he didn't want to go back to Mark and say the bad news. He sat and rested his back on the trunk of a large tree while tears rolled down his cheeks.

He hadn't lost hope of finding Chris, however, and decided to look for him tomorrow under the light of the sun.

James headed back to the cabin and when he got there, he saw Mark sleeping on the couch.

He was glad to see him safe.

Then, he walked to his room. James had no trouble sleeping, given how exhausted he was.

However, he had many nightmares that night, with all of them involving Chris and his escape from the avalanche.

CHAPTER 5

James had only one thing in mind the moment he woke up: Chris. He had to find Chris.

He woke up early and made breakfast for Mark. Before he left the cabin, he left a message for Chris' friend telling him to have breakfast and not to worry because he was going to be back soon.

However, he actually spent more time out than he expected.

Under the light of the sun, he was capable of seeing the full extent of the damage. The avalanche was enormous and could have destroyed the cabin easily.

He looked everywhere for Chris and even excavated some snow in a spot where he found one of Chris' shoes, but he was still nowhere to be found.

He screamed Chris' name as loud as he could, but he got no answer. By noon, he had started to accept that Chris was dead.

Looking defeated once again, he headed back to the cabin and found Mark on the couch.

"Morning, Mark," he said with a fake smile on his face.

Mark didn't say anything and just looked at him.

"I didn't find Chris," he continued, "but I haven't given up hope yet. Neither should you. We will find him, I'm sure of it."

For the rest of the day, neither of them left the cabin. Mark spent most of his time reading a book. James decided to sit on the couch and wait for rescue.

Nevertheless, no rescue came to save them that day. Once it was dark, James had to tell Mark what the two of them already knew.

"I don't think anybody is coming here today, Mark," he said, "but there's no way nobody won't send help. Jelly will surely call the police if we don't return by next week."

Mark, silent the whole day, at last said, "I ho- hope so. I don't want to stay here anymore."

With sadness in his eyes, James could only look at him.

Then, he made dinner and the two of them ate in complete silence. No one could say anything. The howling wind outside dominated the atmosphere.

The second, third, and fourth days after the avalanche brought no good news for James and Mark.

The latter had finally beaten the initial shock and could leave the cabin.

With the teenager by his side, James continued to look for Chris. However, the more he looked, the more he accepted that he was dead.

Nevertheless, he never once said that aloud to Mark. The kid never asked him about Chris, also. He already knew his friend was most likely not alive anymore.

Then the following day came, when his wife would be expecting their return. James and Mark spent most of that day outside, where the rescuers would be able to find them more easily.

The rescuers did come looking for them, but up in the helicopter, they didn't see James and Mark on the ground.

The cabin wasn't on maps and was hard to spot from the sky. Several pine trees surrounded the place.

James and Mark never gave up and continued hoping for a rescue. Even though more helicopters flew over the area, they never found the two men on the ground.

James realized that his lack of preparation and safety precautions might have sentenced him and Mark to their deaths.

He should have told Jelly where the cabin was. He should have told the police where they were going.

However, he never did any of that, and those thoughts began to consume him.

The more time he spent on that mountain alone with Mark, the more he blamed himself.

His personality began to change quickly. Mark began to notice the changes. James was not a charismatic man anymore.

He grew increasingly distant and more violent. He stopped cutting his hair and beard. Furthermore, he frightened Mark.

James became paranoid and prohibited Mark from leaving the cabin. He had also completely given up on finding Chris.

After four months in the mountain, James had stopped talking about Chris. Mark became something he ought to protect at all costs, although he never said that aloud.

He didn't have to. The relationship he developed with Mark was more than enough to make that clear.

Alone and stuck with an increasingly crazy man, Mark could only hope that the situation would change soon.

His hopes, however, were shattered slowly during the following three years.

CHAPTER 6

Three full years had passed since they went to the mountain. Three. Fucking. Full. Years, Mark thought.

He was now an adult. At the age of 18, he was finally taller than James.

The old man, however, had become crazier and paranoid. Mark could still not leave the cabin. James feared for his safety. He didn't want to lose the only person he now knew.

They never celebrated either of their birthdays. How could they? The cold, the long nights and the lack of food killed any good mood they had.

When Mark woke up the day he turned 18, he knew he had to make a decision. He felt like he should leave the cabin and try to return to the city.

However, he didn't know if he had the mental fortitude to go against James. He had grown stronger in the forest. He looked even scarier than in the first months they spent in the mountain.

James didn't look human anymore. His physique made him look like a bear. He was big, hairy, and dirty.

A twink like Mark could only rely on strategy to take down James. If he failed, the crazy man wouldn't stop before he ended up killing him.

Mark knew he had to make a decision, however. He couldn't live like that anymore.

He wrote down the choices he had on a piece of paper and deeply considered the ramifications.

The words listed them as follows:

Stay with James: he would have to endure the paranoid man, maybe for the rest of his life, given that the mountain was always covered in snow. Ever since the avalanche, tourists had stopped coming to the region and he hadn't seen helicopters flying over after the first few months he got stuck there.

Escape: he would have to prepare some kind of trap for James or leave the cabin when he was out hunting. Could he do that, though? He asked himself. Mark knew he couldn't make a single mistake to be successful with that plan.

Kill James: end it there and escape without having to worry about being captured by the crazy man. However, he had no idea he could make himself kill the only person who dedicated the last 3 years to protect him. He knew that James meant well, even though he didn't understand anymore that they should leave the mountain.

After looking at the piece of paper, Mark made a decision.

CHAPTER 7A

Mark wasn't strong enough to stand up to James. The latter was the only person he knew over the last three years. He took care of him and made sure he had everything he needed. He couldn't betray the person that truly loved him.

His feelings for the rough man changed. Under the heat of puberty, he began to admire his chiseled abs, hairy chest, and strong legs.

When the latter was out, he constantly found himself masturbating. He thought of James every time his hand stroked his cock.

One day, when James came back from hunting, a dead hare in his hand, he found Mark fully naked on the couch. His legs were wide open and he was stroking his growing cock.

"I love you," Mark said.

James looked surprised, but he knew it had been years since the last time he had a nice ass under him. He tried to contain the sexual feelings he had developed for Mark, but seeing him there, naked on the couch, destroyed all the barriers he had built around them.

James took off his jacket and positioned himself on top of Mark. He kissed the young man and said, "I love you too."

Their kiss was very passionate. They were releasing years of love they had developed for each other. James was cold and could feel how warm Mark was.

James kneeled on the floor and put the full length of Mark's cock in his mouth. It was relatively big for a man of his age.

He sucked it slow initially, cherishing the virgin instrument in front of him. Mark closed his eyes and moaned.

James scooped the sack in front of him and massaged Mark's testicles.

His technique was rough, but James didn't have to do much to make Mark reach his climax. In a matter of seconds, the young man's cock was throbbing.

Mark blew his load inside James's mouth, and the older man swallowed every drop. Not one drop got away from his hungry lips.

James grabbed Mark and made him stand up. Then, he kissed the young man's lips another time.

Afterward, he made Mark position himself on all fours. The young man opened his butt for the rough guy behind him.

James spat on his hand and massaged the tight hole in front of him. Mark moaned.

Once he felt that the hole was ready, he began to pump the twink in front of him.

"Keep going, keep going," Mark kept saying. James didn't stop. He kept pumping that warm ass.

The older man's initial pace was slow. He knew it was Mark's first time. The latter wasn't used to having a rod inside him.

Mark felt how gentle James was. He remembered the charismatic, happy man that James had been. It was then that he realized he could change James and make him remember the man he was three years ago.

James sped up and pumped Mark harder when he felt that the young man had gotten used to his cock.

Mark felt James' balls constantly hitting against his ass.

Minutes went by until James reached his climax. His cock started to pulse and he got out of Mark's tight hole.

"Look at me," he commanded at the twink in front of him.

He got on his knees and readied himself for the cum shower. The first rope came out in high speed and hit his right cheek. Then, one after the other, James painted the young man's face.

Mark swallowed what he could and lied down on the floor. He had a smile on his face and looked happy.

He had finally come to terms with his life. He craved James, and the latter wanted him as well.

CHAPTER 7B

Mark loved James. He was looking outside, admiring the strong man cutting wood for the fireplace. However, he was done living in the place. He needed to leave.

He had come up with a plan. He was going to get James' keys from his belt and lock him inside the cabin. Then, he was going to run away as fast as he could.

James was done cutting the wood and was heading back inside. He looked a bit exhausted and sweaty.

Mark took off his clothes and headed toward James' bedroom. He planned to get the keys once the old man was sleeping.

James got inside and found it strange not to see Mark on the couch. Fear raced all over in his heart as he shouted, "Mark, where are you?!" But he got no answer.

For the first time in years, he felt alone. He feared Mark had left the cabin and died just like Chris. He opened every door in the cabin until he got to his bedroom and saw the most unexpected thing.

Mark was on the bed, fully naked and his hand stroking his rock-hard cock. He had an evil smile on his face.

"I love you, James," Mark said.

An avalanche of emotions hit James. His hidden, desired feelings for the young man finally resurfaced. He took in the curves of the twink before him, and his dick started to swell.

He took off his heavy pants, and Mark dropped to his knees. He began to massage his member and suck his balls.

James closed his eyes and moaned. The little man was good at what he was doing.

Mark put the full length of the cock in his mouth and felt the top of the head hitting the back of his throat. He felt how pleased James was; it had been years since someone had serviced his instrument like that.

The young man sucked the member harder, and James put his hand on Mark's head. The first began to dictate the rhythm as Mark obeyed his master's desires.

It didn't take long for the alpha man to reach his climax. He blew his load inside Mark's hungry mouth, and the young man gulped down everything.

Some of it spilled onto the floor, and he used his hand to get it. He lapped the cum off his hand and made a "Hmmmm!" as he approved the taste.

He really enjoyed the salty taste of James' white honey.

Mark went back to the bed and positioned himself on all fours. He widened his asscheeks for James, and the latter opened a bright smile. He guided his rock-hard cock into the innocent's hole in front of him and began to pump the young man's sweaty butt.

Mark screamed in pain during the first few seconds, but quickly got used to the size of the member inside him. James began to pump him harder and faster. Mark could only moan in pleasure.

It was the first time James was penetrating a man, and he realized how much he missed a nice butt under him. Mark was tender. His hole was very tight.

In minutes, James reached his climax once again, and he pumped his cum in Mark's hole. The young man moaned loud and slow.

Mark was tired, but James still had the energy for more.

"Move to the side," the latter said angrily.

Mark obeyed with a nod, and James proceeded to suck on the young dick in front of him. He swallowed the pre-cum and scooped the soft sack with one of his hands.

Mark moaned and moaned. His eyes were shut.

James sucked on the pepper-hot dick and felt that Mark was

close to his climax. Slowly, he massaged each of the young man's testicles.

Mark's cock throbbed and he blew his load inside James' moist mouth. The rough man swallowed everything. Not one drop was wasted.

Once they were done, James was fast asleep and snoring. Mark crawled out of the bed slowly and grabbed James's keys from the belt on the floor.

He locked the door to the bedroom, put his clothes back on, and left the cabin. He knew that he was safe for the time being, and then followed the trail to the main road.

Some of the snow that was blocking the trail had melted and he was able to get to the other side of the path with some effort.

Mark wondered how badly Chris' death affected his mind. He was blind to the fact they could already leave the mountain.

Half an hour later, he was already at the main road and heading back to the city.

He shook his arms and screamed at the incoming cars until one stopped. The driver was a kind, old man. He took Mark to the city without asking for money.

He did ask Mark why he was so far from the city at that time of the night. The young man told a fake, yet believable story about how his car had broken down during his trip to the mountain.

His old man made no further questions. Mark was relieved that the driver did not push further to find out more about him.

The young man took a bus to his house, rang the doorbell, and was greeted by people who had thought he was dead.

As for James, he managed to leave the cabin after kicking the locked doors with all of his strength. He quickly found out Mark was not in the mountain anymore.

Once he realized he had lost his protected one, he fell into complete madness. He abandoned the cabin and refused to get near it.

Tourists that visited the area talked about a scary, shadowy figure that roamed between the trees. The police were constantly called to investigate the sightings, but they never found James.

Mark never forgot the three years he lived alone with James in the cabin, but he managed to live a happy life and even married a loving husband.

Every time he left his house and walked outside, however, he kept looking behind him out of fear of seeing James.

CHAPTER 7C

Mark suspected James had feelings for him, but he needed to be sure before he tried anything. He knew the old man had the habit of sleeping like a rock.

He decided he was going to take advantage of that.

James came back from hunting as usual and made dinner for the two of them. At about midnight, he went to his bedroom and left the door open.

Mark could hear him snoring like a pig. The old man had nothing except for his boxer briefs. His bulge looked huge and the twink could not stop looking at it.

Slowly, he crawled to the side of James and began to caress the bulge. James made some noises, but Mark was confident he was not going to wake up.

He slid down the boxer briefs and began to stroke James's cock. His manhood felt soft, sweaty, and sticky at the same time.

It didn't take long for his dick to grow harder.

He put the head into his mouth and began to suck it slowly. James made more noises, but Mark didn't stop.

Once the young man felt more audacious, he started sucking the full length of James' cock.

Unexpectedly to Mark, the cock began to throb violently and ropes of milk filled his mouth. He swallowed what he could, but some of it spilled onto the bedsheets.

Mark crawled out of the bed and didn't slide up James' boxer briefs. He wanted the old man to know he had been there.

Mark was sleeping like a rock when he woke up to someone

slamming open his bedroom door. James had kicked it, but instead of looking angry, he had a smile on his face.

A crazy, wild smile that would have made anyone scared and run away.

Mark was groggy, but he responded to James with a loving smile.

He knew his plan was working. He was going to pump the old man and use his knife under the pillows to end James's life.

Mark was fully naked. James positioned himself on top of the twink. His cock was fully hard and he penetrated the young man fervently.

Mark screamed at the first few thrusts, but quickly got used to losing his virginity. He shut his eyes and moaned loudly. The bed made squeaky noises.

Mark put his hand on James's asscheeks and said, "Harder, harder, please" and the alpha man obeyed. He pumped the tight hole under him faster than before.

In minutes, James reached his climax and released his juice in Mark's moist orifice. He emitted a long moan of pleasure.

The twink was not done and said, "I want to ride your big dick now."

James laid on the bed and Mark guided his hole to the rock-hard cock under him. The rough man began to pump him up and down.

James put his hands on the soft asscheeks over him and began to plunder the twink harder. Mark could only moan in pleasure. James liked dominating weaker men, he thought.

Minutes later, James was pumping his milk into the young man's hole another time. Some of it dripped onto his hips, and he used his hand to swallow it.

James said, "Fuck me now, dear," and positioned himself on all fours, his hairy asscheeks exposed to the young man's eyes.

He guided his cock into the old man's hole and began to pump him. James shut his eyes and moaned in pleasure. Mark grabbed the knife and the man under him did not notice it.

Mark was enjoying the moment, so he continued pumping

James. He sped up his pace and the old man began to moan louder.

Minutes later, he neared the knife to James' neck and thought about everything that had happened to him ever since they got stuck in the mountain.

James was a caring man. He took care of him when he was most vulnerable. Never once did he forget to make breakfast, lunch, or dinner for the young man. He made sure Mark always had what he needed.

Even so, he was tired of living in that cabin and he wanted to get out, even if he ended up dying in the attempt. He wanted to see his caretakers another time.

The current James was never going to understand that. He was a crazy man and still thought they couldn't leave the mountain.

It had been years since the avalanche, and enough snow had to have melted already. Mark believed he could leave that place and return home.

There was only one way he could leave that place safely. James had to die so that his escape wouldn't end in a complete failure.

Mark made up his mind and closed his eyes. The knife slashed multiple times at James' neck. The old man screamed initially, but Mark could not hear anything else after the initial stabbings.

James had also stopped moving.

Mark opened his eyes and looked at James. His blood stained the bedsheets. The young man was sad but full of hope. He knew he was finally going to leave that mountain.

Mark got dressed, picked up the bag he'd brought to the cabin three years ago, and buried the knife far away. He didn't want anyone to find out he'd murdered someone.

As he suspected, the snow had melted and he had little difficulty leaving the mountain.

When he got to the main road, no cars were driving by for him to take a ride to the city. He walked for an hour until he reached a payphone and called home.

The man who raised him picked it up and said, "Hello?"

Tears blurred Mark's vision and it took him a couple of seconds to respond, "It's me."

He didn't hear anything from the other side of the call for a good thirty seconds. Then, he asked, "Mark, is that really you? Oh my God, where've you been? We thought you were dead. We tried-"

Mark interrupted him and said, "It's me. I can't explain what happened right now. Come pick me up at the intersection between Daves Avenue and Morrington Street. I'm by the payphone."

Mark was still crying when the ones who raised him came to pick him up. They were all also crying, but the tears were due to how happy they were feeling.

Mark wasn't dead, and he came back. That was all that mattered to them during that unusual night.

Mark explained half of the events that happened to him and lied about James. He told them that James had died trying to save Chris and that he had been stuck the whole time in the mountain, unable to return home because of the avalanche.

They had no reason not to trust his fake story. Their lives were happy after that night.

Years later, another avalanche rolled down the mountain and buried the cabin. A noisy group of tourists barely escaped the event. The mass of snow hid what was left of James' decaying body, and nobody ever found it.

Mark never fully forgot the murder he committed, but he managed to live a successful life with his caring husband.

The End

If you want to read the other books in the series, check them out here:

1. Old Friend: A Straight to Gay MM First Time Story
2. My Dear Professor: A Straight to Gay MM First Time Story
4. Taken by Brats: A Straight to Gay MMM+ Ganging Story

Lastly, leave a review if you liked the book. It always helps me so much!

STRAIGHT TO GAY SERIES AND MORE

SERIES – EXECUTIVE SUBMISSION

1. Hard in the Office 1: A Straight to Gay MM Story
2. Hard in the Office 2: No Pity for the Miserable Incel
3. Hard in the Office 3: An Incel's Tale of Degrading Humiliation
4. Hard in the Office 4: Bending the Incel Boss
5. Hard in the Office 5: Taming the Incel Spy
6. Hard in the Office 6: Lectured by the Boss

SERIES – OBEY ME

First time gay peppered with age gap.

1. Prep School Obedience 1
2. Prep School Obedience 2
3. Prep School Obedience 3

Other related stories

1. Filthy Wish: A Gay Man of the House on Younger Man Steamy Story
2. Tight and Clenching: A Man of the House on Younger Man Steamy Story
3. Ganged, Used and Devoured: 5 Man of the House and Brat Story Bundle
4. Subdued by the Gay Sitter: Helping the Man of the House
5. Subdued by the Gay Sitter: His Bully's Humiliating Submission

6. Subdued by the Gay Sitter: The Straight Quarterback's First Time

7. Subdued by the Gay Sitter: Straight Jock is put in his Place

8. Used by the Man of the House: 3 OBSCENE Brat Stories

ABOUT THE AUTHOR

Michael Levi's biggest passion? Writing steamy, romantic stories that leave his readers panting. He's currently focusing on ABDL MM romances, but his collection is diverse and there are books for everyone's tastes. If you're looking for straight to gay, first time, BBC, sissification, and more, you're going to find them on his author page.

He lives to pamper his readers, every kiss means a lot more than what meets the eye, and he loves his Alpha males. Making sure that every gay first time feels different, Michael Levi writes his stories with a cup of coffee by his side. And for inspiration, he always opens up a photo of his new crush.